MARGRET & H.A. REY'S
Curious George
Visits a Toy Store

Illustrated in the style of H. A. Rey by Martha Weston

Houghton Mifflin Harcourt
Boston New York

The text of this book is set in 17-pt. Adobe Garamond.
The illustrations are watercolor and charcoal pencil, reproduced in full color.

Library of Congress Cataloging-in-Publication data is available for this title.

ISBN: 978-0-547-49949-9

Manufactured in China
LEO 20 19 18 17 16 15 14
4500719279

This is George.

He was a good little monkey and always very curious.

Today was the opening of a brand-new toy store. George and the man with the yellow hat did not want to be late.

When they arrived, the line to go inside wound all the way around the corner. When a line is this long, it's not easy for a

little monkey to be patient. George sneaked through the crowd.
All he wanted was a peek inside.

George got to the door just as the owner opened it.
"This is no place for a monkey," she said.

But George was so excited he was already inside!
Balls, dolls, bicycles, and games filled the shelves.

There were so many toys—

George didn't even know
how some of them worked.

And how about these hoops?
What did they do?

George was curious. He climbed up to pull one out of the pile.

It would not move.

George pulled harder.

Still it wouldn't move.

George pulled with all fours.

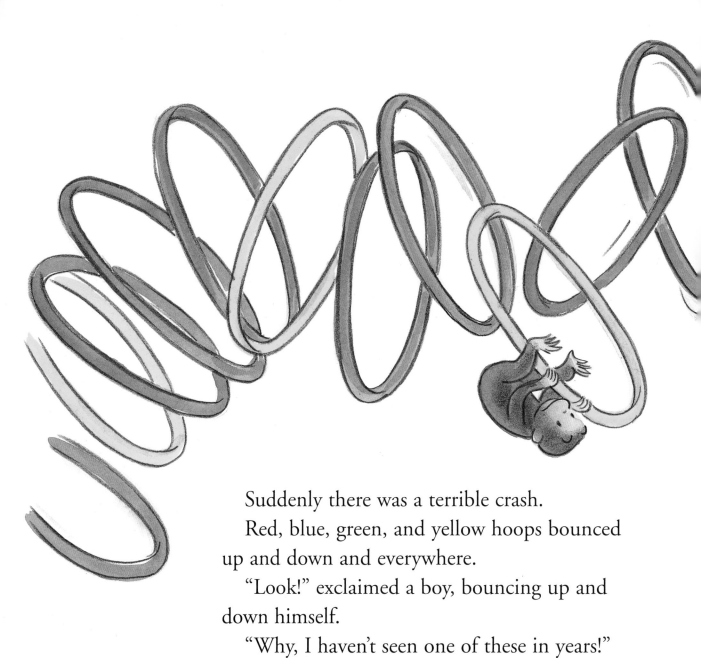

Suddenly there was a terrible crash.

Red, blue, green, and yellow hoops bounced up and down and everywhere.

"Look!" exclaimed a boy, bouncing up and down himself.

"Why, I haven't seen one of these in years!" said the boy's grandmother.

She put a hoop around her waist and gave it a spin.
George tried the hula hoop, too!

Then George pretended to be a wheel.

He rolled and rolled and. . . .

Oops! He rolled right into the owner.

The owner shook her head. "I knew you were trouble," she said. "Now you've made a mess of my new store."

Again she tried to stop George.

And again George was too quick.

In only a second he was around the corner and on the highest shelf.

Below him, George saw a little girl point to a toy out of reach. "Mommy, can we get that dinosaur?" she asked.

George picked up the dinosaur and lowered it to the girl.

She was delighted. So was the small boy next to her. "Could

you get that ball for me, please?" he asked George.

George reached up, grabbed the ball, and bounced it to the boy.

"May I have that puppet way over there?" asked another girl.

18

How lucky that George was a monkey! He swung off the shelf, hung on to a light, picked up the puppet, and put it right into her hands.

"What a show!" shouted a boy.
The children held up their new toys
and cheered. What a commotion!

Immediately the owner came running,
and then came the man with the yellow hat.
"I think we've had enough
monkey business for one day,"
the owner frowned.

Just then a girl got in the long line to pay. "What a great store," she said. "What a great idea to have a little monkey helping you," her father told the owner.

"I guess you're right," the owner replied, and smiled.
Then she gave George a special surprise.

"Thank you, George," she said. "My grand opening is a success because of you. Perhaps monkey business is the best business after all."

The end.